Edward Poste

Bacchylides

A Prose Translation

Edward Poste

Bacchylides
A Prose Translation

ISBN/EAN: 9783337077372

Printed in Europe, USA, Canada, Australia, Japan

Cover: Foto ©Andreas Hilbeck / pixelio.de

More available books at **www.hansebooks.com**

BACCHYLIDES

A PROSE TRANSLATION

BY

E. POSTE, M.A.

FELLOW OF ORIEL COLLEGE, OXFORD

London

MACMILLAN AND CO., Limited

NEW YORK: THE MACMILLAN COMPANY

1898

Oxford
HORACE HART, PRINTER TO THE UNIVERSITY

PREFACE

SOME lovers of poetry, not readers of Greek, may glance with interest at a profe tranflation of the odes of Bacchylides which have been recently recovered from Egyptian papyri. They will hardly need to be warned that all, or nearly all, the poetry is inevitably wafhed out. of a profe tranflation: even if—a large affumption—it retain the fubftantial tiffue of the poet's thought. All brilliancy of diction and harmony of rhythm of courſe diſappear ; indeed, even in verſe, only a tranſlation into Italian or Spaniſh could reproduce, or make any approach towards reproducing, the many-fyllabled epithets and ſonorous cadences of the Greek. Some fragments, too imperfect to intereſt the general reader, have been omitted.

Bacchylides, who flouriſhed between 500 and 450 B.C., was a native of Ceos, the modern Zea, as alſo was his maternal uncle Simonides. Both were rivals of Pindar, and were placed by ancient critics on a liſt of the nine greateſt maſters of lyric poetry.

CONTENTS

The following ode celebrates a victory in the horse races at Olympia won by Hiero, tyrant of Syracuse, at some period between 500 and 450 B.C. The same victory is the subject of one of Pindar's extant odes. What Hiero had to do with Hercules or Meleager is a question which must be left to the conjecture of the reader, as to which the translator can offer little or no assistance. There were doubtless tragic incidents in the career of Hiero; and Bacchylides, after remarking that no human prosperity is unalloyed, proceeds to relate that even the invincible son of Zeus had certain adventures far from joyous.

HIGH-DESTINED lord of car-borne Syracusans, thou canst rightly judge, if any living mortal can, the violet-crowned Muses' dulcet strains: and now, resting awhile from cares of state, turn hither thy attention, and

I   B

pronounce whether the low-cinctured Graces helped to weave his lay the gueſt who comes to your famed city from Zea's ſacred iſle. A votary of golden-filleted Urania he fain with his own voice would ſing the praiſes of Hiero. High aloft cleaving the deeps of ether with fleet tawny wings, the eagle, meſſenger of Zeus, wide-ruling thunderer, boldly travels, confident in matchleſs might, where leſſer warblers fear to venture. Neither peaks of the vaſty earth nor dangerous billows of the ever-reſtleſs main ſtay him, but onward through the abyſs of heaven with fine-ſpun plumage he ſweeps, his ſole companion Zephyr, con-ſpicuous to mortal gaze. I too have myriad paths, by the grace of dark-haired Victory and of brazen-mailed Ares, to celebrate your praiſes, Oh illuſtrious ſons of Dinomenes; on whom may heaven never ceaſe to ſmile.

Cheſtnut-hued Pherenicus, ſtorm-footed ſteed, was witneſſed victorious by golden-fingered dawn both by the fair ſtream of Alpheus and on the haunted meads of Pytho : and by holy Earth I swear, never dust from rival hoof has foiled him when he neared the goal. Fleet as the north wind's blast, and docile to the rein, along shouting nations he speeds winning victory for hospitable Hiero. Call a mortal happy to whom heaven metes a share of triumph, an envied station, and a life of pomp : absolutely blessed there is none of earth's children.

Even he who levelled many a hostile tower, the unconquerable son of Zeus who hurls the flaming thunderbolt, descended, they say, to the infernal halls of fair Persephone, to drag from Hades to the light of day the iron-jawed monster, whelp of deadly-fanged Echidna. There he saw the souls of hapless mortals by the waters of Cocytus, like leaves that the north-west wind drives up and down the sheep-browzed spurs of Ida. Among them gleamed conspicuous, wielding a spear, the lifelike form of a dauntless warrior, grandchild of Porthaon.

Him in refulgent armour noting, Alcmena's heroic fon brought the fhrill-twanging cord to his bow's curved tip, oped his quiver and took thereout a brazen-headed fhaft; when forward ftepped the fhade of Meleager, and thus addreffed him, knowing whom he faw: 'Son of mighty Zeus, ftay where thou art, and with ferener mind forbear to vainly launch a hoftile bolt at fouls of the dead. No foe confronts thee.' So fpake he. Aftonifhed ftood Amphitryo's princely fon, and cried: 'What mortal or immortal fire—what region—reared fuch a fcion? and what hand flew him? Peradventure fair-cinctured Hera will fend the fame adverfary againft my life. But that is a concern for Pallas of the yellow hair.' Him answered Meleager, his cheek bedewed with tears: 'Hard it is for mortals to bend the refolution of the gods. Elfe had car-borne Oeneus allayed the ire of high, flower-crowned, white-armed Artemis, fupplicating, fond fire, with facrifices of many goats and many tawny-

4

hided oxen. But unappeafable was the wrath of the goddefs. She fent, huntrefs maiden, a monfter boar of undaunted fiercenefs into the lovely dales of Calydon; where, refiftlefs in its might, it felled orchards with its tufks, flaughtered fleecy flocks, and every mortal it encountered. With it we, picked band of Hellas, waged defperate battle for fix days without ftay; and when high heaven gave Aetolia victory, we fet ourfelves to bury thofe whom the tufked monfter had flain in furious onfet, Ancaeus and Agelaus, beft of my dear brothers born of Althaea in the far-famed halls of Oeneus. But ftill more warriors were doomed to fall, for the offended huntrefs daughter of Latona had not yet ceafed her wrath, and we joined fierce battle with the valiant Curetes for the boar's tawny hide. There among many others I flew Iphiclus and good Aphareus my mother's gallant brethren. For fierce Ares makes no diftinction of friend or foe, but fhafts fly blindly at oppofing ranks, carrying death wher-

5

ever fortune wills. The sore-stricken daughter of Thestius remembered not this, and—ah hapless mother—resolved my death—ah passion-governed woman. She dragged from rich-carved casket and kindled the quickly burning brand that at my birth fate doomed to be coeval with my days. At the moment I was stripping of his arms Clymenus, valiant son of Deipylus, a youth of noble build, whom I had overtaken outside the walls, when the Curetes fled to the goodly towers of ancient Pleuron. A sudden faintness seized my soul; I felt my strength decline, alas; and with latest breath wept to feel life's youthful splendour flitting.' Men say the eye of Amphitryo's fearless son then and never else was moistened by pity for the ill-starred hero, as thus he answered: 'Mortals' best fate is never to be born nor ever to behold the sun's bright rays. But nought avails repining: so let my tongue frame words to mould the future. Remains there in the palace of Oeneus, dear to Ares, any virgin daughter of features like to thine? Her would I gladly make my honoured bride.' Him anſwered dauntleſs Meleager's ſprite: 'In her father's houſe I left the ſweet-voiced Deianira, unacquainted yet with mortal-charming, golden Aphrodite.'

White-armed Calliope, ſtay here thy ſhapely car. Be now thy theme Zeus, lord of Olympus, ruler of gods; the ever-ruſhing flood of Alpheus; royal Pelops; and Piſa, whence far-famed Pherenicus returned victor in the race to Syracuſa's towers, bringing to Hiero a ſure token of heaven's favour. Truth requires us to puſh envy from our boſom with both hands, and praiſe the mortal who ſucceeds. A Boeotian of old days, Heſiod, ſervant of the Muſes, ſaid: 'The man whom the immortals honour ſhould be honoured by all mortals.' I readily greet Hiero with auſpicious bodings of proſperous career, for that has put forth vigorous ſtems; which may Zeus, moſt mighty ſire, ever guard uninjured by the ſtorm of war.

7

This ode celebrates the victory of a native of Metapontum in a wrestling match in the Pythian games at Delphi. The connexion of the victory with the story of the Proetides consists in the fact that the same Artemis who healed the daughters of Proetus was a deity worshipped at Metapontum and the victor's patron goddess. She derived, according to Callimachus, her title 'Healer of the mind' (Hamera) from curing the Proetides of their moonstruck madness.

[*A few lines, apostrophizing Victory, are wanting.*]

AND on the golden floor of Olympus, stationed by the throne of Zeus, thou adjudgest rank of merit to mortals and immortals. Hail fair-haired daughter of just-judging Zeus! By thy grace athletic youths with choral dance and revelry already proclaim Metapontum a heaven-favoured city; hymning the son of Phaïscus, mark of all eyes, victor in the Pythian games. Him the god whom flowing-robed Latona bore in Delos received with aufpicious glance; and on the head of Alexidamus fell many a wreath of flowers telling of unchequered victory in the rude wreftling match. On that day the fun never faw him fallen on the lap of earth. No, and I will boaft that in facred Pelops' haunted vale by Alpheus' ftream, had only Juftice not been made to ftray from her true path, a pale olive wreath won in conteft againft the champions of all Hellas had encircled his brows when he returned to the nurfe of famous fteeds, his native land. [No malice] in that facred vale affailed the youth with tortuous guile, but or fome adverfe god or erring human judgement wrefted the glorious prize from his hands. And now he owes a fplendid triumph to Artemis the golden-fhafted huntrefs, the healer of the mind, the unerring archer; her to whom the fon of Abas and his fair-robed daughters erft built an altar, goal of many worfhippers.

9

Forth from the splendid halls of Proetus almighty Hera once drove the maidens under the resistless yoke of madness. They with still childish souls entering the sanctuary of the purple-zoned goddess, said that their sire far outshone in wealth her who sits beside the throne of Zeus, majestic king. She in displeasure darted into their bosoms abhorred illusions, and they fled into the mountain forest uttering wild bellowings[1], leaving the towers of Tiryns and its god-built streets. For 'twas there that, deserting heaven-favoured Argos, dauntless brazen-shielded demigods had dwelt full ten years with their all-envied king. For strife implacable from slightest cause had flashed into flame between the sons of Abas, the brothers Proetus and Acrisius. Through them the people whom they ruled were afflicted with civil broils, and partisan tribunals, and slaughterous strife. So they entreated the Abantian brothers to cast lots for the fertile plains, while

[1] 'Proetides implerunt falsis mugitibus agros.'—VERGIL.

10

the younger fhould found the city Tiryns, before irreparable ill enfued. And Zeus, imp of Cronos, in regard for the progeny of Danaus and chivalrous Lynceus, vouchfafed to heal the baleful diforder. Audacious Cyclopian builders coming from afar raifed a wondrous wall for a goodly city, and there the godlike heroes dwelt in high renown, having quitted ftoried Argos, birth-place of fleet fteeds. 'Twas thence the dark-treffed virgin daughters of Proetus fled. Anguifh feized the father's heart, crufhed by the ftrange difafter; and he thought to cleave his breaft with two-edged fword; but his fpearman band with foothing words and ftrong hands hindered him. Full thirteen moons the maidens lurked in darkfome forefts and roved over Arcadia's fheep - browzed glens. But when their fire reached Lufus' fair ftream, after laving in its waters he in-voked crimfon-fcarfed Latona's ox-eyed child, with hands uplifted to the fwift-charioteering fun, to heal his children of their dire falfeweening lunacy—'and I will offer thee in facrifice twenty tawny-hided oxen never yet subjected to the yoke.' The daughter of an almighty fire, the huntrefs maiden, heard his prayer and, perfuading Hera, healed the flower-crowned virgins of their god-forfaken madnefs. They ftraightway enclofed for her a facred grove and reared her an altar, and ftained it with the blood of victims, and inftituted yearly dances of maiden choirs. 'Twas thence that ftarting, oh golden lady of fubject cities, thou wenteft with Achaeans dear to Ares to horfe-pafturing plains of Italy, and, aufpicious fortune in thy train, dwelleft in Metapontum; where they gave thee a lovely grove by the banks of deep Cafuentus in compenfation for thy loft fanctuary, after that by doom of the immortals, leagued with brazen-mailed Atridae, they laid in late ruin Priam's lofty towers. Whofo judges with juft mind will find in every age myriad glorious exploits of Achaeans.

III

On the walls of the temple of Theseus at Athens, according to Pausanias, was to be seen a picture representing the last scene of the adventure narrated in the following ode.

In prehistoric days, before Athens was tyrant of the Aegean, she owed to Crete an annual tribute of seven girls and seven boys to be sacrificed to Minotaur, the Cretan monster.

In this ode Bacchylides assumes that Minos, the Cretan king, has received the tribute; and Theseus, the Athenian hero, in some unexplained position, is on board the vessel which bears them to Crete. The mention of Athena in the opening lines is of good omen for the captives.

Eriboea in after days was mother of the Aeginetan hero, Ajax.

Minos had wedded Pasiphae, daughter of the Sun, as we shall be reminded in the ode.

A BLUE-PROWED ship, bearing valiant Theseus and twice seven noble children of Ionia, was swiftly cleaving Cretan

waters. On its far-gleaming fails fell blafts of
Boreas by the heft of high, aegis-fwaying
Athena. And magic gifts of the charm-
cinctured goddefs Aphrodite ftung the heart of
Minos. He no longer checked a rafh hand,
and touched the white cheeks of a maiden.
But Eriboea fhrieked to the brazen-mailed
defcendant of Pandion. Thefeus beheld, and
beneath frowning brows rolled an indignant
eye, heart-ftruck with keen pain. And thus he
fpoke : 'Son of mighty Zeus, no longer law-
revering wifdom rules thy will. Ufe not, oh
hero, tyrannous violence. Whatever heaven's
refiftlefs doom hath decreed and the fcale of
juftice hath impofed, the utmoft of our pre-
deftined lot, we will fuffer when it comes. But
do thou curb oppreffive purpofe. If a high-
born maiden, Phoenix' fair child, bride of Zeus
beneath the peaks of Ida, made thee by thy birth
moft exalted of mortals; me too the daughter
of rich Pittheus bore to fea-god Pofeidon, and
received as wedding gift a golden veil from

violet-garlanded Nereids. Wherefore, king of Cnoffus, I bid thee abftain from deep-wounding outrage. For I would never willingly fee again the charming light of immortal dawn after thou fhouldeft offer difhonour to any of the youths. Ere that happens we will fhow what ftrength is in our arms, and the iffue heaven fhall arbitrate.' Thus fpoke the hero, armed with juftice. Amazed were the crew to hear his overween-ing rafhnefs; and he who wived the daughter of the Sun was ftirred to anger. He formed an inftant plan, and cried aloud, 'Mighty ruler, Zeus my fire, lift to my prayer. If in footh thou beeft my fire by Phoenix' white-armed daughter, now fend thou down from heaven the fwift, fiery-maned lightning, fignal all may recognize. And if Troezenian Aethra bore thee alfo, Thefeus, to the earth-fhaking god Pofeidon, boldly fling thy fair body into thy father's halls, and bring back the golden ring that now decks my finger from the waves' falt abyfs. Thou fhall fee whether my prayer is granted by the imp of Cronos, lord of the lightning, univerfal king.' Mighty Zeus granted the exorbitant desire, according Minos tranfcendent honour, to give a dear child clear atteftation. He hurled the lightning. Minos, valiant hero, when he faw the welcome portent, pointed towards the vault of heaven and faid : 'Thou feeft, Thefeus, the unambiguous refponfe of Zeus, and now do thou leap into the bafs-voiced waters, and thy fire, the imp of Cronos, lord Pofeidon, fhall give thee glory unparalleled on earth's verdant plains.' So fpake he. The other's courage recoiled not, and ftepping on to the veffel's fhapely ftern he leaped, and the deep received him into its liquid foreft. Then the child of Zeus relented in his inmoft foul, and bade them ftay the fhapely fhip that haftened down the wind. But fate purpofed another way. Onward rufhed the rapid barque, fped by a gale of Boreas blowing from the ftern. All the band of young Athenians trembled when the hero leapt into the waves, and gentle eyes dropped tears from hearts that boded dire difaster. But dolphin denizens of the brine fleetly bore ftrong Thefeus to the palace of his fteed-borne fire. He reached the divine abode, and beheld with awe the ftoried daughters of bleffed Nereus; for their beauteous limbs gleamed with fire-like radiance, and their heads were circled with fillets of woven gold, as with lightly-bending feet they difported in joyous dance. He faw in lovely bower his fire's dear confort, majeftic, ox-eyed Amphitrite; who flung upon him a purple mantle, and on his crifp locks fet a wondrous diadem, erft wedding gift from wily Aphrodite, twined with rofes. Nought willed by heaven is incredible to fober-thinking mortals. He arofe at the fhip's narrow ftern before their eyes. Hah! from what torment-ing thoughts he delivered the Cnoffian king, when, undrenched by the wave, he climbed the fhip's fide, amazing fpectacle, the divine adorn-ments glittering on his limbs. The radiant bench of maidens with new-created courage raiſed a loud cry of gladneſs, the ſea reſounded with the peal, and the boys cloſing round them ſang a paean with ſweet voices. God of Delos, mayeſt thou, charmed by the Zean chorus, grant it heaven-ſent guerdon of applauſe.

IV

The following song for two voices was probably written for the Athenian Ephebi, the youths who garrifoned the frontier fortreffes in their fecond year of military fervice.

One of the fpeakers is Aegeus, king of Athens: the other may be Medea, who fled to Athens after taking vengeance on Jafon.

Procoptes is another name for Procruftes, and Polypemon may be his father.

KING of facred Athens, Lord of Ionians who live at eafe, what tidings caufed the brazen-throated trumpet to found a warlike note? Is a hoftile commander croffing the frontier of our land? Or are marauding brigands, defying fhepherds, driving our flocks in lawlefs raid? Or what alarms thy foul?

Tell me, for, methinks, if any mortal has valiant warriors to defend him, it is thou, oh offfpring of Pandion and Creufa.

A herald came by land from the far end of the ifthmus bringing tidings of wondrous deeds of fome man of might. He flew proud Sinis, ftrongeft of mortals, begotten by him of Cronos born, the earth-fhaker god, Lytaeus : killed the homicidal boar of the groves of Crommyon, and the ruthlefs bandit Sciron: clofed Cercyon's wreftling fchool: and made Procoptes, overmatched, drop Polypemon's heavy hammer. What may be his crowning exploit is my fear.

Who faid he the man was, and whence, and with what train equipped? Said he that he comes with warlike armament and numerous hoft; or unaccompanied, like merchant wandering in foreign lands, but with ftrength and prowefs and daring fingly to overcome fuch mighty ones? Or has he heaven's miffion to bring vengeance on the wicked? Elfe it were not eafy, ever battling, not to meet with a mifhap. In long fpace of time every iffue comes to pafs.

He faid that only two men follow him: that from his gleaming fhoulders hangs a fword [. . . .], two polifhed javelins are in his hands: a fhapely Spartan helm preffes his auburn locks: a purple tunic and a woollen mantle of Theffaly enfold his breaft: his eyes flafh red volcanic flame: he is in youth's earlieft prime: his delight is in the games of Ares, war and battle's brazen clangour: and his feet are bound for fplendour-loving Athens.

V

This ode celebrates a victory at Nemea by a native of Phlius. The river Asopus on which Phlius stood was the mythical father of many daughters who gave their names to various cities and islands, e.g. Thebes, Aegina, Salamis, &c. After touching on the origin of the Nemean games and the victor's deeds, Bacchylides seems about to launch on some Theban mythology when the fragment ends abruptly.

When Adrastus, king of Argos, and the other 'Seven against Thebes' were at Nemea on their march to assist the exiled Polynices to recover his throne, the death of the child Archemorus was recognized by the son of Oecleus, the prophet Amphiaraus, one of the Seven, as an omen of disaster, and he vainly urged his companions to abandon the enterprise.

Achilles traced his lineage, through Peleus, Aeacus, and Aegina, to the river-god Asopus.

22

Amazons from the banks of the Thermodon were said to have fought againſt the Greeks on the ſide of the Trojans.

GRANT, oh golden-ſpindled Graces, perſuaſive ſplendour to the lay which the violet-crowned Muſes' inſpired prieſt prepares to ſing of Phlius and the fertile plain of Nemeaean Zeus: where white-armed Hera reared of old, firſt occaſion for Heracles of glorious exploit, a flock-ſlaughterer, deep-voiced lion. There crimſon-ſhielded demigods, picked band of Argives, held the firſt games over the tomb of young Archemorus, ſlain as he gathered flowers by felon ſnake with yellow-flaſhing eyes, an omen of impending overthrow. Oh reſiſtleſs power of fate! Did not Oecleus' ſon urge them to march back to their warlike homes? Hope often gives ill counſel. She it was who then ſent againſt Thebes Talaïonid Adraſtus, leagued with ſteed-borne Polynices, after thoſe famed conteſts in the fields of Nemea.

23

Illuftrious are the mortals who bind their auburn locks with the triennial wreath. Fortune now hath granted that boon to victorious Automedes, pre-eminent among the athletes of the pentathlum as is among the ftars, when the month is halved, the full-orbed moon : fo goodly a form he fhowed to encircling hofts of Hellas when he threw the rounded difcus; or when the dark-leaved afh's ftem hurled by his hand through the fky called forth applauding fhouts; or when, in the clofing wreftle's lightning flafhes, with the fame tranfcendent ftrength he flung to earth his ftrong-limbed adverfaries ere he returning fought the dark-whirling waters of Afopus. That river's name hath travelled to all regions and as far as the fources of the Nile. Even the dwellers by the fair ftream of Thermodon, fkilled javelin-hurler daughters of fleet-fteeded Ares, rued, oh famous river, the prowefs of a child of thy flood beneath the lofty towers of Troy. To every region on broad highways travel myriad tales of thy race of ample-veftured daughters whom the gods with happy deftiny have feated on the thrones of unconquerable nations. Who hath not heard of Thebe of the hyacinthine locks and her well-built towers? . . .

VI

The ode, of which the following passage is a fragment, celebrated the victory of Pytheas, an Aeginetan, in the boys' pancratium at Nemea. This victory is also celebrated in an extant ode of Pindar.

In the beginning of the ode Teiresias has a prophetic vision of the victory of Heracles over the Nemean lion, and the institution of the Nemean games.

HE shall stay the tyrant's lofty insolence, and give justice to the world. How insupportable a hand the child of Perseus lays upon the neck of the devouring lion with exhaustless resource, when his glittering death-dealing steel cannot pierce the unyielding hide, and the blade bends backward! Truly I predict that spot shall one day witness much-sweated contests of Hellenic champions for the wreaths of the pancratium . . .

Who, ftationed on his veffel's ftern, ftayed bold Hector of the brazen helm fiercely bent, though he was, on deftroying the fhips with horrid fire; what time the fon of Peleus, nurfing wrath, left the field and releafed the Dardan hoft from its terrors. Till then, panic-ftricken, they ventured not to leave Ilion's fair bulwarks, but crouched behind them, dreading the fierce fhock of battle, fo long as Achilles madly raged in the plain, fhattering their ranks with brandifhed, hoft-flaughtering fpear. But when the battle faw no more the violet-crowned Nereid's dauntlefs fon : as on the darkling waters Boreas furioufly affaults with whelming waves feafaring men whom he furprifes refting from their toils by night, but ceafes to ftorm when the light of morning breaks : a calm fmooths the billows : and, the South wind bellying the fails with its breath, the gladdened failors reach the def-paired of harbour : fo the Trojans, when they heard that the grim Achilles was ftaying in his tent becaufe of lovely yellow-haired Brifeis, lifted thankful hands to heaven, feeing war's ftorm-cloud fringed beneath with aufpicious light. Then, leaving with all hafte the walls of Laomedon, they rufhed into the plain, bringing vaft array of war, and ftruck terror into the Danai, urged on by javelin-hurler Ares and the lord of Lycia, Loxias Apollo. They reached the fhore and fought by the fhips' fair fterns, and blood of men flain by hands of Hector reddened the dark foil . . .

. . . They weened that they would deftroy the blue-prowed fhips and all their crews, and that on the morrow the found of joy and revelry would fill the god-built ftreets of Ilion. But fate ordained that, ere that hour arrived, the whirling waters of Scamander fhould be empurpled with their blood as they died by Aeacid hands, overthrowers of their towers . . .

VII

This fragment begins with the story of Io.

THERE are myriad paths of deathlefs fong for whofo has received gifts from the Pierian Mufes, and whofe hymns are clothed with fplendour by the violet-eyed, wreath-difpenfing Graces. Weave now, oh commended Phantafy of a Cean bard, fome novelty concerning lovely, heaven-favoured Athens. Endowed by Calliope with her choiceft gifts, it befeems thee of all others to foar a wondrous flight.

Once upon a time leaving Argos, land of fleet fteeds, Inachus' rofy-fingered child was fleeing far, by the will of mighty Zeus, bleft potentate, tranfformed into a cow with golden horns: and Argus, whofe unwearied eyes looked every way, was bidden by majeftic, golden-mantled Hera, uncouchingly, unfleepingly, to guard the heifer of the lovely horns. Not even Maia's fon could elude his watchful gaze either by the bright-rayed day or the fhades of holy night. But whether fate ordained that the fwift meffenger of Zeus fhould flay the monfter-breeding Earth's fell offfpring, Argus, or his never-refting watch outwearied him at laft, or foothing ftrains of the Pierides clofed his eyes in flumber, my fureft way of fhunning error is only to relate the end. After Io, bearing Epaphus in her womb, had reached the flowered banks of Nile, Zeus made her child ruler of linen-ftoled priefts, lord of peerlefs wealth, and founder of a mighty clan. From Epaphus fprung Agenor's fcion, Cadmus, fire of Semele in feven-gated Thebes. She gave birth to the infpirer of the frenzied Bacchae, Dionyfus [giver of the vine] and inventor of the wreath-crowned dance . . .

VIII

This ode celebrates a chariot victory of Hiero at Olympia, 468 B.C., won the year before his death.

CHOOSE fertile Sicily's queen, Demeter, and her violet-crowned daughter for the theme of thy fong, melodious Clio, and the fleet Olympic-racer fteeds of Hiero. For with tranfcendent victory and grace they flew along the broadly-whirling Alpheus, winning wreaths for Dinomenes' heaven-favoured fon. And Achaean ranks exclaimed: 'Thrice happy man who, by Zeus invefted wideft ruler of Hellenes, has the wifdom not to hide his high-piled wealth behind a dark obfcuring fhroud. The temples are aftir with feftive facrifices of oxen, the ftreets with hofpitality; and bright flafh the corufcations from the gold of deep-

31

chafed tripods, fet before the fhrine where the holieft grove of Phoebus by Caftalia's ftream is miniftered by Delphic priefts.'

Heaven,Heaven demands a tribute from every fortune-favoured mortal. For in bygone days horfe-taming Lydia's monarch, when by Zeus' fatal ordinance Sardis fell before the Perfian hoft, Croefus was protected by the golden-fworded god, Apollo. When the grievous day arrived, the king was not one to await the added woe of a flave's all-tearful doom, but reared a pyre before the brazen walls of his palace-court, and mounted thereon with his confort dear and fair-haired, wildly weeping daughters. And, raifing his hands towards the o'er-canopying heaven, he cried reproachfully : 'Oh, overmaftering fupernal power, where is the gratitude of all the gods? Where is Latona's princely fon?
. . . [Lydian blood ftains] the golden-fanded Pactolus. Lydian dames are ignominioufly torn from well-built homes. The hated foe is henceforth to be their dear lord. No! death is

a fweeter lot.' So faying he bade kindle the gorgeous-carpeted wooden ſtructure. His daughters ſhrieked and flung their hands about their mother's neck: for horrid to mortals is the face of imminent death. But when the fierce fire's gleam began to penetrate the pile, Zeus brought overhead an abyſs of darkſome cloud, and quenched the yellow flame. Incredible is nought that the divine will works. Thereupon the Delian god Apollo bore the old king to the Hyperboreans, and enthroned him in their midſt with his taper-ankled daughters in requital of his piety, becauſe that of all mortals he had ſent the richeſt offerings to god-haunted Pytho . . .

King Apollo, the herdſman god, once told the ſon of Pheres: 'Mortal as thou art thou muſt nurſe two expectations: that to-morrow's ſolar ray is the laſt which thou ſhalt ſee; and that thou ſhalt count another fifty years of happy life.' Live righteouſly and joyouſly; this is higheſt wiſdom. The wife will underſtand theſe words : The depths of ether have no ſtain ; the water of the ſea no corruption ; gold is cheerer of the heart; and to man it is not given to caſt off hoary eld and recover youthful days. But virtue's radiance dims not with the mortal frame's decay. It is nurtured by the muſe. Hiero, thou haſt ſhown the world proſperous fortune's faireſt flowers. A bright career receives not his due meed from ſilence ; and one of thoſe who aim aright will be he who ſhall ſing the honeyed ſtrains of the Cean nightingale.

IX

This fragment relates to the demand addreſſed to the Trojans for the reſtoration of Helen. The Grecian embaſſy was introduced by Antenor, of whom we read in Vergil: 'Antenor potuit mediis elapſus Achivis Illyricos penetrare ſinus.' His ſons were worſhipped as heroes at Cyrene. They give the ode its title, Antenoridae.

THEIR ſire, prudent hero, bore to royal Priam and his ſons all the meſſage of the Achaeans. Then heralds ſpeeding through the wide-ſpread city ſummoned the Trojan tribes to the people's meeting-place. Everywhere ran the tidings loudly-voiced, and hands uplifted to the immortal gods prayed that their troubles ſoon might have an end. Say, Muſe, whoſe tongue firſt urged the plea of right. Pleiſthenid Menelaus uttered winning words counſelled by the fair-robed Graces.

'Oh warlike Trojans, it is not high-ruling and all-feeing Zeus that is the caufe to men of their calamities; for all mankind are free to hold faft to ftraight-walking Juftice, companion of chafte Order and wife Law. Happy they whofe children choofe to have this dweller in their ftreets! But fhe who flourifhes by treacherous falfehood and bold contempt of equal meafure, nought-reverencing Arrogance, firft lightly gives away another's wealth and havings, and after plunges into deep difafter. She it was that brought annihilation on the overweening race of Earth-born giants . . .'

X

The following fragment shows that the plot of the Trachiniae, a play which some attribute to Sophocles, others to Iophon, his less-gifted son, had been already outlined in the verses of Bacchylides.

SUCH was the strain that Delphic choirs sang before thy far-famed shrine, oh Pythian Apollo. Already Oechalia, said the lay, had been left a flaming ruin by Amphitryo's dauntless son, when he touched at the Euboean promontory, purposing to offer from his spoils nine deep-voiced bulls in sacrifice to cloudy-throned Kenaian Zeus, two to the god who lifts the sea and shakes the earth, and to Athena, stern-eyed virgin, a single heifer, unyoked, lofty-horned. Then an overmastering power inspired Deianira with a plan, that cost her many tears, to recover her consort's love, after ſhe heard the cruel tidings that white-armed Iole was on her way, ſent under eſcort to his palace as a lovely bride by Zeus' dreadleſs ſon. Ah, hapleſs wife! Ah, evil-ſtarred! How direful was her deed! Malevolence of a mighty one wrought her ruin, and darkneſs ſhrouding future days, when on the ruſhing waters of Lycormas ſhe took into her hand's a fatal gift from Neſſus. . . .

XI

Before the discovery of the papyri the following fragment was the longest remnant of the poems of Bacchylides.

FOR mortals Peace has blessings in her hands, plenty and poesy's nectared flowers. And for the immortals thighs of oxen and long-fleeced sheep burn in yellow flames on rich-carved altars. Athletic sports and the flute and festive dances busy the young. But in the shields' iron-bound handles the tawny spider weaves her webs, and the long-shafted spear-heads and double-edged swords are marred with rust. Nor is the brazen clarion heard frightening sweet slumber, soul-caresser, from the eyelids. But joyous revelry fills the streets, and notes of love-songs tremble in the air.